A Song of Truth and Semblance

A Song of Truth and Semblance

A Novel by Cees Nooteboom

Translated from the Dutch by Adrienne Dixon

Louisiana State University Press

Baton Rouge and London   1984

Library of Congress Cataloging in Publication Data

Nooteboom, Cees, 1933–
    A song of truth and semblance.
    Translation of: Een lied van schijn en wezen.
    I. Title.
PT5881.24.O55L513   1984   839.3'1364   84-848
ISBN 0-8071-1176-7

O this is strange deception. Subtle and false exchanges of
what is real and what but seems.

Frederik van Eeden
The Song of Truth and Semblance, III

A Song of Truth and Semblance

"That is what a writer must do, of course," said the writer. "Hover like an eagle above the characters he wishes to pursue. In this case the doctor and the colonel."

"So they do exist?" asked the other writer. "You work from existing people?"

"They exist from the moment you invent them," answered the writer, who was not sure of this at all. The conversation bored him. How could he explain to the other writer that he saw before him neither the doctor nor the colonel, that he had just invented them, during the conversation, merely to be rid of the harassment (about their craft, my God, and why don't you *do* anything these days). In the empty space where his thoughts were at present wandering—a station concourse, a hospital waiting room, a sports hall—he vaguely discerned the outline of a military figure. Epaulets, rather operettalike. So the story could either not be set in the present time, or not in our continent. For who wore such epaulets here and now?

"How old are they?" asked the other writer.

The writer did not reply. Did he know it was a barracks because he had seen those epaulets? In the empty mess hall in the barracks he saw the stethoscope passing by, accompanied by nothing, nobody. The object floated, at human height, through the air. But what was this doctor doing in the barracks?

"What does a doctor do in a barracks?" he asked.

"Visit his son," said the other writer, whose own son was doing his military service.

"With a stethoscope, I suppose," said the writer petulantly. He saw the epaulets turning toward the stethoscope and, while the instrument remained suspended in total immobility, the right epaulet made jerky movements that were undoubtedly caused by the as yet invisible arm beneath. Excitement therefore.

Just as he thought he could see the blur of a head, the first manifestation of a face, the other writer said: "What an idea, that you should be writing a story about doctors."

The writer did not answer, for fear that everything might then vanish, and he was rewarded. On the wall behind the epaulets there appeared a portrait, framed and glazed, of a man in uniform, wearing many decorations. The text in Cyrillic script he was unable to read, but he realized it was time to get rid of the other writer.

Two hours after the other writer had left, somewhat offended because of the abrupt farewell (barely civil), the writer was still sitting in the same position at his desk. There is something indescribably sad about writers alone in their studies. Sooner or later the moment arrives when they start to have doubts about what they are doing. It would perhaps be strange if it were not so. As a person gets older, reality becomes more obtrusive and at the same time less interesting because there is so much of it. Is it really necessary to add anything? Must the invented be piled up on top of the existing merely because someone, in his youth when he had little experience of what is called reality, invented some pseudo-reality and was consequently called a writer?

On the paper in front of him, the writer had written only one line: "The colonel falls in love with the doctor's wife."

The utter banality of this sentence made him feel sick. "So what," he muttered. "The colonel is in love with the doctor's wife." Although the writer's lofty prose poems had won him the reputation of a literary aesthete, he was usually fairly coarse in the mouth when among friends. "The epaulets screw the stethoscope's wife. So what?" What business was it of his? No doubt, in all the five continents, there were colonels in love with doctors' wives and doctors in love with colonels' wives—and since colonels and doctors had existed for several hundred years, his story had obviously been written several hundred times—by life itself. On the other hand, that was true of everything. Every variant had already been invented, because it had already been lived. There were writers who thought that a story written by them would clarify something about reality itself, but what was the use? This clarity would merely form part of the reader's reality, and was not the reader, finally, nothing other than a possible subject for a story?

Writers, thought the writer, invent a reality in which they are not obliged to live themselves, but over which they have control. He gave the still so empty sheet of paper a little push. Was that strictly true? Did he have control over those two faces he saw so slowly coming into existence? Or did they have control over him?

The doctor's face was pale and fine-featured (what an invention! As if not millions of pale, fine-featured faces had appeared in the world and disappeared!). But pale and fine-featured it was. Cool, slightly bulging grey eyes that would not change their expression if they saw something terrible, eyebrows and lashes of soft black hair, the mouth almost colorless and somewhat too shapely. The most masculine thing about the face was really the hair that seemed to pour out of the head and caused a growth of beard that probably had to be kept in check twice a day but remained nevertheless present like a bluish haze under the white skin. Something dark under something light, the writer thought, and on the sheet in front of him he wrote: "like water under ice, where nobody has yet skated." He put a question mark after that and crossed it all out again. Something now occupied his mind. If it was a form of power to describe the physique of nonexistent people (to give nonexistent people a physique) based on some internal, unverifiable vision—then the height of that power must surely consist in giving *names* to these nonexistent people, as if they were really registered in the, in a, registry of births.

"Stefan, Stefan, Stefan," said the colonel, prodding the doctor between the two graceful nickel curves of the stethoscope through which had passed the sound of so many death rattles. "Stefan, I swear that this is the end."

That *what* is the end? thought the writer, feeling a slight nausea rising in him. He had stopped smoking two weeks ago and the finger with which the colonel prodded the doctor's chest was amber with nicotine. It was a short, broad finger that represented the colonel's physique perfectly, for although the epaulets had floated a little way above the stethoscope (but now that the massive fleshy figure had filled the empty vision under the gold decorations, there was no longer any question of floating), the colonel, since he had almost no neck, seemed in reality not taller, but on the contrary, smaller than the doctor.

For a while the writer listened, without hearing anything, or rather, without registering what he heard, to the rain tapping on the window, and then wrote: "How can you tell if someone is an admirer of Schopenhauer?" He looked briefly at what he had written, then crossed out the word *How* and changed the *c* of *can* into a capital letter. If someone is an admirer of Schopenhauer, this is a part of his being, and a bit of this, he thought, must surely show on the outside. He wondered. It was already presumptuous enough to have decided that the colonel admired Schopenhauer, but should that admiration be evident from his appearance? Would there, in all that bloodbath of the Balkans (look at that half-imbecile portrait with the Cyrillic lettering, of course it was the Balkans!) have been even *one* colonel who read Schopenhauer? Who had even one single small volume of his most popular aphorisms in the house? And would you then be able to tell it from his appearance? He went to his bookcase, took out a volume of Schopenhauer, opened it at random, shut it again and put it back. Five minutes later he took it out a second time and spent the next hour reading and leafing through it. In the course of that hour Colonel Lyuben Georgiev became an advocate of the monarchy, against noise, acquired the self-image of a cynic, and was unmarried. But of course, he already *was* all these things.

It had started raining outside. Doctor Fičev took his leave of the colonel, who reluctantly let him go. In his room he took off his white coat, returned the stethoscope to its case, and put on his uniform jacket in front of the mirror. I swear that this is the end, it droned on in his head, but what was not the end, for Lyuben? The way he always became excited about everything, this uncynical cynic; he ought to look after his heart. Schopenhauer, of whom in Fičev's opinion the colonel had scarcely read a word, was the greatest philosopher of all time, the Bulgarian past had been feloniously appropriated by the Turks, the Congress of Berlin had been rigged by a bunch of crooks, if this Battenberg was worth anything he would have himself crowned Czar of Bulgaria, why did the Russians rescue us at Pleven if afterwards . . . and so on.

The doctor sighed and caught himself looking at his reflection as he did so, a sighing man in a mirror. Someone not interested in Bulgaria, someone who did not care whether this or that aristocratic German buffoon became king or czar, who actually hated the Russians and would prefer to leave the army and Sofia today rather than tomorrow. But where would he go? To the only country where a man looking like this could go: to Italy. And with a vision of light and palaces and sun in large piazzas he stepped out into the rain. But the thought of Colonel Georgiev would not leave him. Why this hero of the Turkish war, who had played such a large part as early as during the '76 rebellion, a man who was his opposite in every respect, visited him more and more often these days, and why he himself consented to this, even though consent was perhaps not the right word, was a mystery to him, and whether this mystery was pleasant or unpleasant he did not know either. Those piercing, never-yielding black eyes that fixed themselves on you from that broad, much too Bulgarian face like the barrels of guns; the rattling, curt way of speaking as if everyone were his subordinate; and at the same time that strange weakness as if he were being eaten up or pursued by something for which the colonel himself could think of no words or, if he could, words he was ashamed to utter. These were, thought the doctor, the symptoms of people who have been told that they are incurably ill and in whom you clearly see the wish to hit, first of all, the person who had the unpleasant duty to tell them their fate—as if that would do any good.

The doctor paused to let a farm cart pass. Under the yoke in the rain, the white oxen hung their heads. Their feet made soft imprints in the mud that immediately ran into each other like dribble. Bulgarian mud, thought the doctor, at the same time reflecting that the mystery of their relationship lay partly in the fact that he felt that he was Lyuben Georgiev's subordinate. In the colonel's presence he felt himself changing into a servant, someone who constantly needs his master's approving eye, even though he knows a terrible secret about him. But what that secret might be, Doctor Fičev had no idea.

5

The writer now knew more about Bulgaria than anyone of his acquaintance. Not that this was very difficult, since nobody had ever been able to understand the hopeless shambles of the former Balkans, except a few philatelists. Bosnia, Serbia, Herzegovina, Roumelia, all those frontiers dancing back and forth, all those colors roving about the map—as on the *Ethnographische Karte der Europäischen Türkei und ihre Dependenzen zu Anfang des Jahres 1877 von Carl Sax, K.u.K. österreichischerungarischer Consul in Adrianopel*—yellow for the schismatic-orthodox Bulgarians, brown for the Moslem Bulgarians, and all those other whirling colors of the exploded prism, for the Graeco-Walachians, the Greek Orthodox Serbs, the Roman Catholic Serbo-Croats, and then, superimposed, the shifting national borders, each new frontier drenched in useless blood. Perhaps that was the only utility of the story he was writing, that at least *he* concerned himself with it even though he would not use a hundredth part of the gruesome, macabre visions that rose from the maps and pages: forgotten, bygone massacres— the connective tissue of history—suffering of which no one would ever be able to imagine that it had been real, and actually about something.

Suffering, he thought, ought to weigh something, have a specific gravity of its own, be visible like an ore that does not exist anywhere else, an unchanging currency in which the corpses, blood, wounds, sickness, and humiliations are kept and which would remain behind on the battlefields, in prisons, places of execution and hospitals, a monument that would always and everywhere have the same meaning.

With a vague irritation he remembered how a few days earlier he had met the other writer on the way out of the university library. They had had a coffee together and as usual the other writer had pried into his bag to see what books he was taking out.

"Hmm . . . *The Balkan Volunteers* . . ." He had looked through it for a bit and had then leafed through the *Guide Bleu* of Bulgaria, wheedled with considerable difficulty by the writer out of the map room; he had inspected the poorly executed brochures printed in bad colors obtained from the Bulgarian Information Office. "Hmm . . . Bulgaria . . . singularly unattractive country, don't you think? The most faithful vassal of them all, that's why you never hear anything about it. Sofia seems to be rather like Assen. Never been there, don't want to either. Actually, the whole Eastern bloc doesn't appeal to me." The other writer was always so sure of everything. Every year or thereabouts, a novel or collection of stories appeared from his hand, his work was translated abroad and highly regarded at home, he was a member of juries and of the Arts Council, and—what intrigued the writer most of all and made him a bit jealous as well—he really seemed to enjoy writing.

"Bulgarian spas," muttered the other writer, still fishing around in the bag. "Koprivshtitsa, my God, what a language. Are you sure you know how to pronounce it? Are you going there?"

"No," answered the writer curtly, and added with slight nonchalance, "I need it for a story."

The other writer groaned and pushed the plastic bag away from him with outspread fingers. "Better you than me," he said, and they parted.

6

The colonel did not have a high opinion of himself as a soldier, although he would never admit this to anyone. He had witnessed the terrible carnage around Pleven three times, as one of the commanders of the seven-and-a-half thousand Bulgarian volunteers in the Russian liberation army. The summer stench of the bodies, the lacerated carcasses of horses, the half-rotted soldiers, still with bayonets poking up into the empty air, all these gruesome details that you saw and then again did not see, the cloven heads in which a sword had remained stuck, mud on bodies, worthy, stupid, ridiculous, and spliced bodies, somehow these images had slipped away, vanished from his memory after every lost battle.

The long months of waiting and hanging about in the camp of the Russian general staff he had spent doing drill and reading Hilendarsky. That had been written more than a hundred years ago, but no one had ever evoked the glorious Bulgarian past so vividly, and sometimes the colonel hoped that the great writer would be in a place from where he could see that today in the 1870s, the great struggle for freedom against the Turkish barbarians had begun at last. But in spite of the fact that on the Sipka Pass and elsewhere he had conducted himself as a hero, and had been decorated as such by the Russians, he had his doubts as to his own cold-bloodedness. It had only been after Omar Pasha's desperate attempt to break out of Pleven that the nightmares, which he regarded as a manifestation of cowardice, had begun to plague him. The screams, the wailing, and the groaning of the Turks trapped in the frozen snow, the tattered bodies of soldiers stranded on their death march to Russia, surrounded by a malevolent cloud of crows—frozen, black clusters in the desolate white plain.

Every night they trekked through his dreams, thirty thousand lost souls leaving behind them a chain of dying and dead men who were then devoured by half-savage dogs and pigs.

Once he had stopped, together with some Russian officers, to watch, seated on his horse, a fight between dogs and pigs over two corpses frozen together. The Russians were drunk and had formed into two parties, the party of the pigs and the party of the dogs. The pigs kept pushing at the twined bodies with obscene upward movements of their snouts; the dogs tugged at the same time, pausing only to wail, high and loud. This and the retching throat noises of the pigs haunted the colonel at night and even caused him to wake up screaming like a pig himself. But then it was dark; the black, flat slab of the Bulgarian night pressed on the land while the images in his dream had possessed the terrifying clarity of things that happen in an unnatural, flashing sunlight.

He was ashamed in front of his orderly, who came to light the oil lamp and looked at him, wild with fright, in a way an orderly ought not to look at a colonel. Long ago, at the military academy where he had been trained, the old Prussian officer who taught him military theory and with whom he sometimes played chess in the evening had said to him once: "Winning is nothing, my boy, winning leaves no trace, it is mere gratification. Losing is living."

The man was accustomed to speaking in paradoxes and Lyuben had therefore simply laughed, but the German—who, incidentally, had given him his love of Schopenhauer—said: "You may laugh! You'll find out one day: at the gaming table, with women, and in war—losing is living, winning is death, because there is nothing afterwards. Not exactly orthodox, and I ought not to say it, but you can stand it. Checkmate."

7

There was no one the colonel could talk with about his night-mares. The only person he occasionally conversed with for longer than five minutes was Fičev, but he shrank from divulging the secret, which he called his weakness, to the doctor, if for no other reason than that you never knew how those cool eyes would look at you. Besides, nothing seemed to excite Fičev except the barbaric conditions in the camp of the Russian general staff.

"Can you imagine," he said, "the Czar of All the Russias in residence and not a latrine in the whole camp. The czar shits squatting on the ground just like the pigs and the dogs and the soldiers in the field. Barbarism starts on our side of the Adriatic; we were born on the wrong shore." And then there followed another lyrical description of Venice, Florence, Rome. He listened with polite absentmindedness to the inspired stories of bygone greatness with which Lyuben Georgiev replied (smuggled out of sight! Simeon the Great! our glorious Middle Ages! Tarnovo! all of it buried under five hundred years of Turkish shit!). The heroic deeds of Kaloyan, the greatness of

Preslav and Ohrid, the frescoes in the Boyana, the last great revival under Ivan Sisman before the Turkish darkness settled for good on the land; none of it seemed to mean anything to the doctor. There was only one civilization, and that was the Latin civilization, the civilization of light. Bulgarians were barbarians, just like the Russians and Turks; the Balkan peninsula was a hell, a seething cauldron of blood shed in stupid and useless wars. All you could do with it was make a huge black pudding, to be shared among the rest of the world to eat.

The terrors of the war had left the doctor curiously untouched. "It was what you would expect in the Balkans." It did not affect him, as if under his soft, bluish-white skin there was a metal armor that admitted nothing. He had carried out operations, sawing, hacking, and listening to the screams beneath him, with the impassivity of a mechanical doll. The colonel, who had often heard the screaming and wailing at a distance, was again reminded of the Turk-eating pigs, and at such moments he hated Fičev because he knew he would be unable to sleep that night.

The few times that he had cautiously referred to the connection between blood, death, war, and nightmares, Fičev had reacted merely ironically. "Listen, Lyuben," he would say, "blood and wounds are your profession. You people always think that you have won when you can ride your horses in a procession, when you have spent a few years on Clausewitz and studied troop movements on those splendid maps of yours—but all those arrows, lines, offensives, and maneuvers have to be translated into wailing Russians, roaring Turks, and your own nightmares, if you have any."

The colonel remembered that moment very clearly. It was in the summer of '78. It was the first time Fičev had allowed the word *nightmare* to pass his lips. They were walking past one of those large iced-cake houses in the center of Sofia. The sun was shining, the weather was hot and clear, and in the distance you could see the mountains with the heavy benevolent mass of the Vitosha rising above everything.

"I have them every night," said the colonel.

The doctor stopped. "You must be crazy," he said. "Drink a grozdova before you go to bed."

"That only makes it worse," said Lyuben Georgiev. "Then I see . . ."

8

Hate was perhaps the best word to describe the feeling that took possession of the writer when he looked at those last three words. "Then I see . . ." Then I see what? he thought, and he knew he would never find out now. Why had he, four months ago, stopped in the middle of a sentence? Telephone, someone at the door, a bout of flu, then a lecture somewhere, a two-month trip to Spain where he had worked on something different, something for money, something contemptible, therefore, because a real writer does not allow himself to be kept from his work. But all right, he had gone away on a journey, he had kept with him as a talisman the exercise book containing his story, in and out of hotel rooms, but he had never opened it again. So his colonel and his doctor had slumbered, frozen at the moment of that last sentence, the colonel with his mouth still half open as if the cutter had interrupted the picture on the cutting table while the word that was to follow "see" remained unuttered in the half-open mouth. The hatred he felt was not the result of the interruption at that particular moment. No, it touched the whole problem: the deceit, the trickery.

The reader (the reader!) would never know about those intervening months, would never know that the random word he would now write in order to continue the story was not the word (was probably not the word) he had intended to write four months earlier. But it would become the word the colonel intended to say, and then that word and no other would immediately be the only word the colonel could have said because it was the word he had said. Whatever he might invent, that invention would become reality to the reader.

9

"Then I see ghosts."

With his eyes the doctor followed a large white dog that slowly, as if at any moment it might lie down for good, walked along in the shadow of the houses, and only when the dog had actually lain down and appeared in fact to be dying, did he say: "Ghosts in uniform, I suppose?"

The colonel's broad hand, already in a cramped grip although holding nothing, descended vertically on the doctor's shoulder and grasped it so firmly that it seemed as if he wanted to squeeze the faint scorn out of the remark, like juice from an orange.

"No, bodies, corpses, stuck together, with holes in them. Bodies with faces that look like mine. Bodies that talk, but I can't understand what they say."

"No one ever dreams of himself," said Fičev. "You dream *about* yourself, you run away, you do something, but you never see yourself."

"They have my face."

"Do you know what you look like? You don't use a mirror even when you shave."

The colonel shrugged his shoulders. He did not like his appearance, so he looked at it as seldom as possible. It did not surprise him at all that Fičev found this strange, because the doctor was like a woman in that respect. He could not pass a mirror without glancing at it, as if afraid that he did not exist.

"Sometimes it drives me crazy," he said.

"What does?" asked the doctor.

For a moment Lyuben thought of hitting him, but he said, "My nightmares. The other day I woke up five meters from my bed with a bleeding head."

"But the war has been over for ages."

"That's just it," said the colonel. "I have too much time to think."

"In this muck-yard there will soon be another war," said the doctor cheerily.

"Then that will be the fault of those scoundrels in Berlin," said the colonel. "If those so-called great powers had not bartered our country away . . . is that what we fought for, to give Nish to Serbia and Dobrudya to Roumania, to those Latin whores?"

The broad hand hovered in the air, a weapon seeking an opponent. Stefan Fičev took a step back. The autonomy of that coarse hand irritated him. The way it moved back and forth before him—an object rather than something that could be called a hand—a thing of flesh and bone that without further orders was bent on destruction. A Bulgarian hand, he thought, a hand that cannot caress, that cannot make light gestures, that can scarcely write properly, and he wondered whether it could be in this hand, and in the colonel who was, after all, attached to it, that his whole aversion to his compatriots was contained, to people with hands that could strangle, but that hid weakness and chaos behind their strength—a chaos (and he thought this was rather a witty thought on his part) that was all the more dangerous when you let such hands loose on it. Once he had seen the colonel pick up by the scruff a dog that had attacked the body of a sergeant he had known well, and throw the animal away so violently with one hand that its neck broke with a quick, dry sound the moment he let go of it.

They crossed a street in silence. Since East Roumelia had remained under the Turks and other parts of the country had simply been given away by a group of gentlemen around a distant, German, round table, the whole business would have to start all over again within ten years, Fičev was right. It did not seem to worry him; he would calmly resume his hacking and sawing as before, letting the screams blow away in the air that reeked of blood. Always talking about art, but hard as steel in the face of the worst brutalities. The colonel did not know that at this moment the doctor was thinking of the hands of Raphael, Michelangelo, and Mantegna. Different hands, hands that had made something, and weren't just good at destroying things.

Fičev looked at the broad figure beside him, at the broad, somber face that was turned to the ground with a look of permanent rage. What binds me to this fool, he thought. One day he must go to Italy with me. Then I shall show him that there are other things in the world than this everlasting slaughter-house full of illiterates. And then I want to *see* his expression. I will spoil Bulgaria for him for good. But he was not really sure whether he would succeed. "I'll give you some bromide," he said and sounded as if he were talking to a spoilt child. The colonel's hand clenched into a fist in his pocket.

"Esse est actus et potentia," said the other writer.

The writer felt annoyed that once again he had allowed himself to be drawn into a discussion. "My Latin is a bit rusty," he said, and he thought: this is what comes of attending receptions where the whole Dutch literary world is present. With aversion he eyed the meatballs and the peanuts in their little glass dishes and the trays of poor, lukewarm white wine, viñasol or paternina or even worse, but at any rate Spanish. One of their venerable colleagues was celebrating his fiftieth birthday. There had been a sudden rise in the number of fifty-year-olds in the Dutch world of letters, a rain of prizes was descending, and the half-centenarians were being fêted as if it were a way of burying them, as if everyone was already convinced, or hoping—that was possible too—that nothing further would ever issue from their pens.

"What does it mean?" he asked.

The other writer, not a beauty at the best of times, looked at this moment even more like a monkey than usual, for he was standing by a potted palm in the winter garden at the Krasnapolski Hotel, stuffing a handful of peanuts into his mouth. A Latin-speaking monkey, my God.

"Esse est actus et potentia," said the monkey through the peanuts. "That is the solution to your entire problem, because it is not a problem. What is, is real and possible at the same time. What you invent is real, because it is *possible*."

"I had got that far myself," said the writer curtly. "The question is only why someone should bother, why an invented reality should have to be added to the existing one."

"I could give you a philosophical answer to that," said the monkey, this time hindered in his speech by an over-hot meatball, "but philosophy is not your strong point, if you don't mind my saying so. If *one* sacred line cannot help you, the whole arsenal won't be any use. You're obstinate, that's your trouble. And that is why I am now going to give you the so-called *straight* answers, the material proof. One, in spite of what you may say, writing is fun. Those idiots who say they suffer so have made it into a masochistic ritual. So for them it's still fun. Two, because you get money for it, and money burns in your hands" (at this, he looked at the writer's pianist's hands as if stigmata could be seen there). "Three, because it makes you famous, and fame in the Netherlands is still worth having. Not because of the fame itself, but, oh dear, the self-affirmation, and four—very important—you have to do *something*, and in my opinion there is nothing else you *can* do. It is amazingly simple, but you keep getting in your own way because you are ashamed of practicing a simple craft, the craft of telling a simple story with a beginning and an end. And yet you have written a few good stories in the past."

27

"Yes, in the past, without really thinking about it."

"Then do it again!"

"Do what?"

"Not think about it. Writing is work. A painter who thinks about painting all day doesn't paint."

"It might add another dimension to his painting."

"If he doesn't paint anything you won't be able to tell."

"Perhaps he does."

The other writer wiped his mouth with his writing hand and said: "Excuses! Nonsense and excuses!" And walked away, leaving the writer to the doctor and the colonel.

11

The peace of San Stefano had been concluded, but the colonel was not satisfied. Firstly because a large area was still held by the Turks and secondly because he did not know what to make of it all. He had said good-bye to Fičev, who had returned to his native town of Tarnovo, and he himself had gone back to his own rooms in the house of Mrs. Zograf, a widow, in the center of Sofia. He went to his club, drank too much, suffered from nightmares, and was bored. The war slowly slipped out of his daily existence and visited him only at night. In the daytime he felt a curious emptiness, which he was unable to fill with his work on the organization of the new national army. Pointless, bloodless exercises with stupid recruits, hierarchical wrangles over rank and promotion, and a good deal of gossip in the nationalistic clubs about the German Battenberg who would never become a real Balkan czar, and that was more or less all. He nursed his resentment against the great powers, missed the doctor, to his surprise, went riding, visited a brothel from time to time, and hoped for a rebellion. When his bromide was finished he thought of writing to Fičev, but it would have been the first letter to anyone in ten years, so he never got round to it. He had taken a long time to finish the bottle because he did not want to ask the new regimental doctor, for although he still had not made up his mind whether or not he liked Fičev, he did at least trust him—and with a new doctor you never knew: he did not relish the thought of tales going around the barracks about the hero of the Sipka Pass who took bromide for his nerves.

A week after the big bottle was finished, a letter arrived from Fičev. It was brief. Stefan Fičev was getting married (the fool) and asked the colonel to be his witness. With revulsion Lyuben Georgiev thought of all the primitive nonsense this entailed, including having to shave the bridegroom. He could just see himself, tending to that horrid beard of Fičev's. However, he couldn't very well refuse.

12

Something mysterious happened to the writer at this point. Excitement, that was the best word to describe it. He did not like the word sexual in combination with excitement, because that suggested a localization of the intensified feeling, whereas the excitement he felt was everywhere, inside him and even around him. It definitely had something to do with the woman, for it had started only after Fičev's letter from Tarnovo. He found a compromise in "sensual," but there again, was that possible: sensual excitement about a nonexistent woman? Not if you are a really good writer, the other writer would have said, but the writer avoided him, successfully as it happened. On the other hand, if his story were a mere fabrication, an invention intended to serve as a reflection of life such as appeared in thousands of books, for the entertainment of the public, would he still have felt this curious excitement? But that woman, whoever she would turn out to be, was surely an invention?

What I want, he thought, but he was not sure whether this too was his own invention or whether he had read it somewhere, is that what I write should be an inverted metaphor of reality. How did that quote from Goethe go again? *Alles Bestehende ist ein Gleichnis.* But why an inverted metaphor? No, he couldn't have invented that himself. To have the written be a metaphor for the existing, and the existing be a metaphor for itself, that was enough for him. As to this excitement, he was sure to get to the bottom of it sooner or later. Drivel, he heard the other writer say somewhere at the back of his head. He said it very airily, as if sitting in a comfortable chair, blowing out smoke, and this time the writer was not altogether sure whether he might not be right. But it was too late now to listen.

13

The colonel came from the Trakijska Nizina, and as a man of the plains he did not like mountains—he always had a feeling they stood between him and the view. Yet he could not entirely escape the appeal of Tarnovo. The river Jantra, which came thundering down from the Sipka Pass, had carved its path through the mountains so sharply that the hills around which it twisted in capricious curls seemed to have become islands. From a distance he recognized the Carevec and the Trapezica and as he approached the town he saw the clustered houses with their red roofs dancing in the unruly mirror of the river. He had the feeling that it was not quite real, too beautiful, more suitable for a painting. Just like Fičev, to come from such a place.

For two centuries Tarnovo had been the resplendent capital of medieval Bulgaria, and it still showed. The image of greatness had never completely disappeared. Even Fičev would have to admit that his famous namesake, the architect, had, in his time, built a number of magnificent—and truly Bulgarian—houses and churches.

But when the colonel and the doctor first met again after so long, they did not talk of that, because Stefan Fičev had brought his intended with him, and she took the colonel's breath away so literally that he, never very talkative, remained silent for the time being.

14

When he later contemplated what had been his first feelings on meeting Laura Fičev, he usually got no further than "homesickness." He was not the man to analyze his feelings, nor was homesickness a particularly clearly defined concept for him (certainly not in connection with people), and yet it appeared to be the only word that could to some degree give expression to the strange emotion that possessed him ever since that first instant and had never left him again, whether she was present or not. But that was not true either—it was worse when she was present.

The only time in his life he had been homesick had been in Germany, at the military academy. Walking back to his quarters from the bar at night, he would see a flat, wide, dusty, summery vision of the plain from which he came. It tightened his throat, and so that was homesickness, a feeling whereby your throat tightened.

Laura Fičev was not like other women in any way. It was as if for her alone a different kind of human being had been invented. There was an almost crazy looseness about her movements. Seemingly the law of gravity did not apply to her. She floated or sailed, slightly above the ground—her manner of moving did not necessarily have anything to do with walking, and this was not the only natural law she violated. Her skin always appeared to catch the light earlier than that of other people so that you always saw her face first, no matter where, outside or indoors, and all her movements—bending, pointing, rearranging something—seemed to be made by a body without joints, without bones, as if she could, should she wish it, curl up catlike—an impression reinforced by the fact that none of these movements ever made a sound. It was rather eerie, in fact. Whenever the colonel looked at her he felt his own body growing heavier, increasing in matter, so that his steps became louder and his movements slower. His reflection in the mirror broadened, his voice sounded harsh in his ears for the first time in his life, and he even had the frightening sensation that the objects he picked up—a glass, a cup, a cigarette— would break at the merest touch. For the first time in his life he mistrusted his body, or rather he felt detached from it; it became a dog that accompanied him everywhere and seemed not altogether trustworthy.

All this happened in the first hour. It was inescapable, and Lyuben Georgiev knew, without putting it into words, that his life had changed, because one does not meet such people with impunity. And this was even before he had become aware of all the other terrifying things: her voice, always surrounded by air, so that everything she said came in separate, veiled parcels of breath, which gave the impression that what she said was not true, or that it was not true that she said anything, or, he thought later, the manner in which she spoke made you think she was talking to someone who was not there. The fact that her blue eyes above the high cheekbones looked right through you as she spoke appeared almost normal by comparison. Her hair was thick and blonde, the only thing about her that gave material confidence, her hands long, very white, almost translucent. The colonel scarcely dared touch those hands.

15

"Inverted metaphor? Why not perverted metaphor?" There was something petulant in the other writer's voice, which might be talking to a fractious child that refused to understand that piano lessons were good for something. "I still can't see why you're willing to dig ten meters deep into all kinds of silly theories but not to tell a simple straightforward story. But I feel as if I've already said this a thousand times. Read Trollope, Fontane, or if you like, Sir Walter Scott or Graham Greene. Surely you needn't be ashamed of the tradition from which you stem? The distance between now and then may seem great, but it isn't really, and with all that gimmickry you don't please anybody. You'll lose your readers by it, if you have any left. Readers can be driven away in two ways. One: by a lack of craftsmanship, and two: through being bored by the craft as such. Whether writing is an ordinary metaphor of reality or an inverted one means nothing to your reader. The only thing that interests him is whether what he reads becomes reality to him at that moment. Or rather, *is*. If it is not, he rejects it, if the critics haven't already done so before him. The trouble with you," he was about to add, "is that you don't like writing," but it was neither the place nor the moment to start that kind of truth game, for the two writers were walking side by side in the funeral cortege of a third, who preceded them in the anthologies.

Strange, that they should be walking side by side, but it seemed as though at such moments a unity of opposites arose— they had at least one thing in common, their aversion to processions, marches, togetherness. The last time that they had walked in a procession together had been at the great Cambodia demonstration, and without knowing about the other, each still saw one moment of that afternoon clearly before him: when the procession turned the corner of the Reguliersbreestraat and Halvemaansteeg, and the chants that had already sounded so strange and loud in the broader streets suddenly started to rebound back and forth in the narrow alley: "Nix-on mur-der-er, Nix-on mur-der-er, Nix-on mur-der-er." Both of them had felt rather unhappy and at once sought each other's company. Neither had ever before been in a demonstration, and it was not as easy as they had thought: the red flags, the unfurled banners, the chants, led by men with stirring voices. The sentiments they endorsed but not the volume, intended to reach as far as Washington. To anyone standing by the roadside that afternoon they both looked like mere crowd, because they formed part of the crowd, but the soul does not become a member of the mass so readily. Later, when history, which itself sometimes resembles a demonstration, had also turned a corner, the writer occasionally thought of that march. The regime they had helped to power by means of that march of theirs (for you have to look at it that way, otherwise you would have to

39

admit that such demonstrations serve only one's own soul and are therefore useless and then you might just as well not join them) had by then already murdered more people than had previously been killed in bombings, and the writer had felt it necessary to walk along the route of that long-past march again, but this time *alone*, by way of meditation, as a penance, a pilgrimage, he did not quite know what, perhaps as an expression of mourning.

Mourning was definitely not what he felt at the funeral of his colleague. Dutch writers cannot as a rule do much for each other, but they do bury each other very well, and if ever there was an inverted metaphor of reality it was a funeral of this kind, which resembled a literary ball more than anything else. The everyone-is-there syndrome, the curious relatives whom you would never have imagined as having anything to do with the deceased (authors have no relatives), the awful anecdotes about the dead man and the slight feeling of elation at walking so sadly down the gravel path, the prospect of undrinkable coffee and the drinks afterwards—all this mingled with wafts of real grief for the other and for yourself—the surprise at recognizing gnarled old essayists and white-haired poets whom you had presumed to have been residing in the realm of the dead for years, the whole "business," as the other writer called it, gave you a fleeting feeling of unity, which was bearable only because everyone knew it would fall apart an hour later into separate quarterlies, coteries, trends, and lonely scribblers, mostly in rather curious rooms invisible to the world.

One sentence in the obituary of the deceased, who had not

been a great author although an industrious one, whose novels would in all likelihood not make it to the end of the century, stuck in his mind. "He created his stories by projecting his inner world onto the external world, without actually intending to 'depict' his own person."

What, thought the writer, as the first relatives were already beginning to return from the graveside in the opposite direction, is my inner world in the case of Fičev and Georgiev? Or don't I have one? The only indication was that somehow or other he had imagined those characters himself. But that was precisely the terminology he detested. He had seen them. Or hadn't he?

"Do you think it is possible," he asked the other writer, who was clutching a bunch of white narcissus as if he had to pulverize them before they got to the grave, "to put so much of yourself into a few randomly chosen characters from a period you know hardly anything about, that something is revealed about yourself? I mean, the point of the whole idea would then, in my view . . ." but they had arrived at the grave and he caught no more of the other writer's answer than: "Telling a story and nothing else, and any other motivation . . . to be sorted out by students of literature . . . as far as I am concerned . . . could drop dead (which sounded somewhat crude at the place where they were standing) . . . better in ten thousand homes than . . . a couple of academic nut-cases . . . Nymeghen University . . . don't care a fig."

Together they looked briefly at the hole in the earth in which the pale-gleaming coffin of their forever silent colleague was waiting for the eternal darkness that would start five minutes later. The other writer threw the narcissus onto the wooden lid and they turned around.

"Your reader merely wants to know what happened to that colonel, and as far as he is concerned your precious inner world has nothing to do with it."

Then, after a long minute during which they looked at their earth-smudged shoes on the crunchy gravel, he added grumpily, "If they haven't lost interest by then."

No, conversations with the other writer did not always run smoothly.

16

That night, in his hotel, the colonel had several things to think about, but because these were so enigmatic he did not know where to start thinking. He realized he had fallen in love with Laura Fičev, or rather, with the woman who would from tomorrow on be the wife of doctor Stefan Fičev. So this swaying, burning sensation was being in love, a ridiculous state for a man in his forties to be in. He had never experienced it before, and it had hit him like a shell burst—he was unable to think of a more interesting comparison. But what was far more mysterious to him, so mysterious that he began to doubt his common sense, was that his love was requited, flagrantly, ostentatiously, deadly seriously.

At a given moment the doctor had left the room and Laura Fičev had come toward him, Lyuben, before he had managed to formulate, with difficulty, some utterly trivial remark, and with that voice that seemed to flow not from her face but from a different corner of the room, she had said something like: "I know, yes, I know"—and then she had made one of her bird-like tours of the room and had paused by the window, a suddenly very quiet figure in grey silk against the dark-brown curtain. Light entering from outside had made her face even paler, and from under the wide helmet of blonde hair her blue eyes had looked at a different Lyuben, someone he perhaps *was*, but who was not altogether inside him, but rather somewhere half beside, half inside him, so that he was no longer sure whether those words she had just spoken had been addressed to him. Then, in another of her quick, unpredictable runs, she had come toward him, had touched his face and, just before Fičev entered, whirled away soundlessly.

He thought he would suffocate, and he was also quite sure now that he was afraid of her, because she was mad, and even surer that her hand was still visible on his face, like a sign. But although this was not true (it is very rare for hands to be visible on faces), Stefan Fičev did notice his confusion, and seemed not displeased by it. A Dutch writer had once claimed, almost a hundred years after these events took place, that a man's choice of woman expresses his attitude to life—or words to that effect —and so it was exactly, thought Fičev. He had chosen Laura because of the effect she would have on others, and especially because he would see that effect. Not that he remained untouched by it himself, but the fact that the effect was so visible formed the essence of his feelings for her. To himself, he had called Laura un-Bulgarian, perhaps even anti-Bulgarian, and the first person on whom he could try this out was his beloved antipode Lyuben Georgiev. The poor fellow had toppled head over heels, that much was certain, and Laura, too, seemed curiously affected. This was actually much more difficult to explain, for what a woman could see in a clumsy hunk of flesh like Lyuben was a mystery to him. However, it made it all the more exciting. The doctor was one of those people for whom jealousy is an indispensable ingredient of love, and he took this to great lengths. If the jealousy did not occur spontaneously, it had to be engineered. Whether or not Laura had noticed anything of this and was playing with him, he was unable to say. It was too early to tell, and moreover, he had already given up trying to interpret her reactions. Not quite right in the head, he often thought, with a certain satisfaction, and he attributed her odd behavior to the fact that she had suffered from tuberculosis for many years. She had been officially declared cured, but she was still always either very tired or in a state of scarcely controllable rapture, the cause of which was not always clear. But it was precisely this alternation between her fragility, and languor, and then again that floatingness, and that almost-madness that fascinated him so. If he could persuade Lyuben to go with them to Italy, everything would be as he wanted it. Not only would he then have an audience, but he would also constantly be able to feel that extra excitement that was already there now to some extent. And moreover, that Bulgarian block of ice would surely have to melt at last, in the Mediterranean light, and admit what Fičev had been telling him for so long: that there existed only one country on earth. And it was not Bulgaria. He counted the days till the moment when he could finally leave this pigsty.

17

Colonel Georgiev loathed everything that was Turkish, but that night he smoked at least a hundred Turkish cigarettes, until he felt as if his whole mouth had been carved to bits by the thin, sharp tobacco. He had tried to sleep, but since Laura Fičev had begun to haunt even his nightmares like a ghost roaming about a battlefield, it had been no use. He would wake up in a sweat, pace up and down the stuffy room like a condemned man who is to be executed in the early hours of the morning. He opened the windows. Cool mountain air and the deathly silence of Tarnovo poured into his room, but it was all to no avail. The feeling of threat would not leave him. At the wedding he would look like a man of fifty who had not slept all night and has tried to rinse out the taste of pungent cigarettes and the fear of his own dreams with too many glasses of bad peasant brandy.

If only there had been someone he could talk to, even if merely to a Dutch writer, but the only Dutch writer who knew him fairly well had not yet been born, and besides, the colonel was unable to talk. He had never done it in his life.

The only person to whom he had ever tried to tell anything about himself was Stefan Fičev, but it had merely resulted in that shameful bottle of bromide that was now empty. And what occupied him at the moment he would never be able to talk about to anyone, least of all to Fičev.

When during shaving, contrary to his habit, he looked at his reflection in the mirror, he saw his bloodshot eyes and thought: I look like a pig and I am as stupid as a pig—and as this sentence pleased him he repeated it aloud a few more times, between the echoing bathroom walls.

Snatches of the conversation during dinner went through his weary brain—the whole evening had been a compact lump of all their former discussions. Fičev had forced him to be more Bulgarian than ever, and he had clamored so loudly for a rebellion in East Roumelia that there had been applause from nearby tables. When finally, in a loud voice, he had started raking up memories of their joint heroic deeds—all the easier since the gruesome setting he needed appeared nightly in his dreams —the proprietor had offered them a bottle of Crimean champagne.

My God, he who never said anything, what a fool he had made of himself! Yet it had not failed to make an impression on Laura Fičev. She had sat at the table like a trembling reed, and during the silences in the increasingly noisy conversation of the two men she had even told some stories herself. Exotic stories, about things and places he did not know, and no matter how hard he tried to follow it all, he had not succeeded. Ballet lessons with a famous teacher in Paris, a sanatorium in Switzerland and the life one lived there. He had not been able to form a picture of it, not even when she spoke of the other patients and of the high, white mountains all around. The idea that she had spent so many years among other sufferers . . . would they have been people like her? Her father had been an ambassador, or had worked in embassies . . . Stockholm . . . Rome . . . He might perhaps have been able to understand her if she had not kept stopping halfway through one story to start another, so that strange fragments of her incomprehensible life darted feverishly across the table, fragments of which he was unable to grasp the significance but in which he would have wished to lose himself utterly, had this been possible. At times he wanted to clutch the edge of the table to stop himself stretching out his hand toward her, or in order not to be sucked into that turbulent disintegrating throng of incomplete memories.

Again and again he saw before him that moment when she had brought her face so close to his—but however intently he looked at her, the face of that afternoon did not return, no, as he reflected on it, it seemed as if she had not looked at him once all evening, unlike Fičev, who stared at him all the time, like a contented tomcat that has eaten rather too much of his favorite food.

18

A story like this could end only with the death of one or two of the main characters, or perhaps even of all three. But he still had not figured out what it meant if you made a fictitious person die.

"Nothing," said the other writer, "as long as it is part of the logical cohesion of your story. Not if you have to do it to get rid of someone or to bring something to a conclusion, like bad playwrights who send a character offstage with a message because someone else has to enter and say something he is not supposed to hear."

"But that is not what I mean," said the writer. "I mean . . ."

" . . . metaphysically," the other completed mockingly. "The divine omnipotence of the creator and all that nonsense!"

Goodness, how frequently these Dutch writers meet. This time they met in the corridor of their publisher's office. The writer looked enviously at the fat parcel of proofs which the other writer was carrying under his arm.

"It isn't as difficult as all that, you know," said the other writer, lifting the fat packet of print with a theatrical, but swift movement high above him and letting it land with a heavy smack on his balding head. "This is where it all comes from, and if I'm lucky it will find its way into twenty, forty thousand others." They walked along the Singel, separating to avoid cars and then coming together again, past the Athenaeum bookstore, where three different titles by the other writer were on display in the window, and on to Arti, the famous artists' club that stood as a bastion of nineteenth-century calm overlooking the Rokin.

"We look quite impressive like this," the other writer said, when they were seated in two large Berlage chairs.

"Have a glass of wine, then I will try to explain it to you for the last time. Look, I am not such a fool that I don't understand what you are talking about. But you have been talking about it far too long, and besides, it is something you should concern yourself with only at the beginning of your . . . your career, let's call it that. Writing is a funny business and if you think about it too much you don't write any more. I always pretend I am a twentieth-century village storyteller, and of course that is nonsense too, but I have decided that it is a craft and that I exercise this craft without supernatural speculations. A world exists and I tell the world about that world. This can be done in many different ways and I have chosen a very simple but fairly intelligent way, because that is what I happen to be good at. People read me because they recognize something, perhaps even because, paradoxically, they recognize something they didn't know yet, and that is enough for me. I don't experiment with style because nothing gets old and moldy as quickly as language; even if you write very simply it gets threadbare before you die. Only very few writers escape that, and even if they do, it remains to be seen for how long. Beyond that I do not philosophize about what I do, because in my opinion the philosophy should be *in* what I do. That is me. You're quite different. You think the world only begins to exist when you start writing. You, a man who doesn't want to write—for I assume that someone who hasn't written for so long doesn't really want to write—you believe in this much more than I do. For if the world only begins to exist when you write, you really mean that *you* only begin to exist when you write. And that means," he said not without satisfaction, leaning back in his chair, "that you keep having to decide over and over whether you want to exist or not. It is not the reality of your characters that you doubt, but your own. If you can invent someone, someone may have invented you."

The writer did not reply. He always hated it when, as he called it, people were practicing psychology on him, and this he called his need for invisibility. No one had the right to examine him and he could not really imagine that anyone would do so and then form an opinion about him. Life was complicated enough already, without others interfering, and they only made it worse if they got hold of his thoughts and if these were not his real thoughts.

"To feign the truth in order to be nothing," said the other writer, not without pedantry, in a tone of someone quoting. "Do you know who wrote that?"

"Pessoa." The writer said it with difficulty, as if having to admit a fault.

"Look, perhaps you won't like what I am going to say to

you now," continued the other writer as he rubbed himself comfortably against the capacious round back of his chair, "but I don't want you to get angry with me. Pessoa sacrificed his life on the altar of literature. An hysterical cliché, but that is what it comes down to: you only need to read his letters. And if I were to be really asinine now, I would say: that is *his* business. A great poet, but to put it bluntly: a pathological case. I always wonder whether literature is worth it. You can also make it sound very lofty and say he was so afraid of not existing that, all the while smoking and drinking, he divided himself into four poets, so as to make sure that he had existed when, paradox paradox, he no longer existed. And he succeeded, too! Through his material life he created an immaterial oeuvre that still exists. The only thing he was able to enjoy materially as he wrote and drank himself to death was that prospect. His greatest creation was his life, but first it had to be completed."

"Nonsense," said the writer. He liked Pessoa and he hated theoretical discussions. "If he had led the same life but had written bad poetry, we would not be talking about him. Besides, there is always the pleasure of the activity itself."

"But you can't deny that he created his life as a fiction and himself as a character in a novel that could be comprehended only when the novel was completed."

"Perhaps, but the difference between him and a character in a novel was that he did have to live his own life first."

"All right. Now you yourself have stated the difference. Hurrah. Your constant, fruitless preoccupation is whether people in books do or do not exist. Pessoa was not a person in a book. He had to live every second of his life materially, and he could have lived differently, not drinking, getting married, not writing, burning his poetry, anything. He had a choice. And that is the difference from characters in books, because they do not have that choice. Someone else, the writer, has it instead. And that is why people in books do of course exist, and of course do not exist. When I said to you once: 'I could give you a philosophical answer,' that is what I meant. If I say a person in a book does not exist, I mean he does not exist materially. 'Form without matter exists potentially, not actually.' Aristotle. And this potential existence is what happens in books."

It now seemed as if the other writer was having difficulty with the conversation too, for a hint of sweat crossed his already gleaming, pedantic forehead.

"Look," he said, "there you have the exact boundary of the existence of a character in a book. Pessoa more or less chose his own life. You might say at any rate he chose, let us say, his own life from a certain moment onward. You, for instance, can still die a thousand deaths. Madame Bovary can and could die only one death, always the same. If your hero dies on page two hundred and six, it is always in the same way, just as he will always, when I read your story today or my son reads it in twenty years' time, pick a rose on page twenty. Did der junge Werther exist, or for that matter, does he? Yes, whenever someone reads him. He exists each time you read Goethe, each time you think of that suffering young man, or use him as a concept. But his existence consists of words that have never become flesh. He does not consist of matter, any more than Don Quixote and Lolita. And I shouldn't say this to you, because it will only confuse you further, but if you want to know more about it—my knowledge in this field has become rather rusty, thank God—go to the library of the Theological Institute, Herengracht 514, and ask for Thomas Aquinas and go down the rope ladder into the depths of actus and potentia. You'll be doing your readers a great service." And as if this were his last word, he closed his eyes and began to chant, with an ultra-Catholic intonation, the great church father's *Tantum ergo*. But not for long. Their publisher entered and offered to get them a drink, returning a moment later with a gin for the writer and red wine for the other writer, who fixed his eye pensively on the large Breitner painting diagonally opposite him.

"Good old Breitner," he said approvingly, and as if the rest of his sentence followed logically, he continued, "Now I am to make a fool of myself. Pessoa once again." And he quoted, as people do when they want to express a negative opinion about the lines they are quoting, with a slightly theatrical inflection, like a comedian:

> *Could it be that we on earth are but pens and ink with which someone truly writes what we are scribbling here?*

Very nice, and yet it is nonsense, and very irritating, in fact. *Why* should it be someone else? Always that fascination with not really existing, not really writing, being a double of, being written by, not having existed. Take Borges, for example. True, he is far less sentimental than Pessoa and he writes with a show of awesome lucidity, as if it is all very rational. Splendid, oh yes, beautiful fairy tales, high above the tree line of most other writers, but nonsense all the same. I wouldn't like to say so in an article, because then the whole world would be down on me."

He drained his glass in one draught, looked with feigned entreaty at the publisher, and said: "Another?"

The publisher stood up without a word and walked the long distance to the bar.

"He'll be quite some while," said the other writer, assessing the queue the publisher had to join, "because I wanted to say something very disagreeable to you, and there is no need for him to hear it."

He pressed his finger against the middle of his forehead as if to put a secret sign on it, and said: "What I mean is this: For that kind of highly intellectual exercise you need caliber, and you don't have that. Neither have I, but I know it. You don't even know it, and that is what's wrong. Down there, with Pessoa, it hurts, and up there, with Borges, it is cold. Very very cold."

"I never wanted to be there," the writer said, suddenly thinking how odd it sounded. "It's just that I wonder about certain things. I wonder what exactly someone is doing when he writes a story, and surely that is the least you may wonder about. And besides . . ."

But the other writer had already moved on to something else and said, "The crazy arrogance that writers have! Every writer thinks he is different, and preferably better, than other people, because he looks at them and then creates yet other people in their and his own image and likeness, as if he had somehow or other swallowed up the essence of people and is therefore in a position to share it out. If you forget for a moment the pious prattle of the cultured middle classes, you know that the majority of people are about as interested in writing or in the art of writing as they are in bridge building or in pre-historic archaeology."

"If that is so," said the publisher, returning with the tray and putting the glasses on the table, "there are gloomy days ahead."

19

"The masses think very little, because they have neither the time for it nor the practice." The colonel had read this in Schopenhauer, without wondering whether it could perhaps apply to himself. Someone who read Schopenhauer did not, in his opinion, belong to the masses, and so that took care of that. About God, just to name someone, Lyuben Georgiev had never really thought at all. But now, because of all the strange things that were happening to him, he suddenly had the feeling—that soft beginning of thought—that somewhere, in some place or other, some invisible intelligence doubted his, Lyuben's, existence, and he began to doubt God's existence, in the sense that he began to wonder whether a God could exist who was different from the solid block of nothingness you needed to swear the officer's oath on, or to spur your soldiers into action. This invisible Thing, which in an equally invisible way had something to do with the state, now that they had one, and therefore with the army, seemed to have become interested in him. It is a fact that most people do not like doubting their own existence, especially when they have never done so before. But by dragging in this invisible Authority Lyuben Georgiev solved nothing for himself; on the contrary, his nightmares and his daytime confusion became worse. He woke up four or five times a night and could not remember if he had dreamt of Laura, or Fičev, or of the war, or of all and everything at once, and it therefore seemed as if the nightmares went on in the day. Her image was the same, night and day, or, rather, even in the daytime Laura Fičev was someone who was scarcely there, who weighed almost nothing, as if the matter she was composed of were lighter than anyone else; the sound of her voice dissolved even as she spoke; he still had to make an effort to follow her. But worst of all was her way of looking, as though she lacked the strength to sustain her gaze and therefore fixed her eyes on the empty space beside someone, so as not to have to close them at once.

He had endured the wedding with difficulty; at the sight of the crown above her immensely pale, absent face, he had trembled, overcome with fear that she might suddenly collapse or perhaps vanish altogether. Amid the incense and the sonorous chants he had felt that there was nothing left of the Georgiev he knew, that he was fast wasting away. He no longer recognized himself, not when he made an effort to think about himself nor when he looked in the mirror and saw an idiot in uniform, looking miserably at him and pointing one finger at his forehead as though to burn a hole in it.

Whether he would go to Rome with them, as Fičev had suggested, he did not know. To pile something even stranger on top of all this terrifying strangeness seemed the biggest mistake he could make. If he did go, he would first have to arrange his leave and replacement in Sofia, and that would take at least a week.

He could not imagine that Fičev had noticed nothing of what he himself called his "folly," and he did not really care any more, because with Fičev you never knew what he thought anyway, and besides, the doctor spoke of his beloved with the same cynicism as he did of all other topics he had ever talked about with the colonel, except Italy.

"She attracts me because she is ill," he had said. "Ill and mad at the same time. Can you imagine that? No, you can't, can you, Lyuben, you old cavalier. That, according to Schopenhauer, of whom you have read no more than I, which is nothing, is what I have halved my rights for and doubled my duties. I think Schopenhauer must have been henpecked pretty badly by the ladies, hahaha! He's right, actually, except in my case it's different!"

The colonel thought, but did not say, that when Schopenhauer had been talking of women he could not possibly have meant Laura Fičev. She fell outside all categories. Outside all categories? He found it hard to formulate for himself what he meant by that. "No woman is any good." Surely that could never refer to her! Perhaps in the first place she was something else, a being of another order, different from all the other men and women he had ever known. Before he had, by this coercive circuit, arrived at the angels, the doctor again interrupted his painful train of thought and said, crudely as usual, "When I go to bed with her I always think she'll kick the bucket."

All this happened while they were on a walk. Ash-grey clouds, loam path, delirious flowers, forceful river, foaming waves, distant mountains. The colonel stopped.

Oh God, thought Fičev, there is that big hand again.

But the hand described a semi-arc through the air, hovered hesitantly for a moment like a planet that has lost its moon, and then sank away into the void.

"Is that going too far for you?" said Fičev with satisfaction. "It is actually the reason I married her. I knew it the first time I saw her. She's mad, I thought, but you won't find such madness anywhere in Bulgaria. She usually talks nonsense that as a rule I don't follow, and when I lie in bed with her I don't know half the time whether she knows I am there. Exactly what I want."

The big hands clenched, but the colonel said nothing. They continued their walk along the path by the river. The light hurt their eyes.

"Why do you want me to come to Rome with you?"

Fičev laughed his usual malicious little laugh.

"I knew you were going to ask that."

"People don't usually take a third person with them on their honeymoon."

"But Lyuben, you're not a third person! We have seen death together!" And then there followed a Slavonic embrace, which the colonel knew to be more like a Judas kiss than anything else. This was no kiss, this was a wrestling match between two large animals for the privilege of each other's hairy cheeks, and in Fičev's case there was even a disdainful coolness about it.

"I will explain something about my character to you," said

60

the doctor, "because you need to have everything explained to you. When I have had a good dinner somewhere, although I don't know where that could have been, in this country of dogs and peasants, I want my friends to dine there too, I have a domineering nature."

It seemed as though Fičev was actually getting a little sentimental.

"God, Lyuben, how many friends does a man have? Because I know you don't believe me, because I know you think it is all nonsense, I want to ram it into that thick Bulgarian head of yours just for once what it means: art, civilization, light. We shall eat on terraces, we shall walk along the Tiber just as we are now walking by the Jantra, we shall see more art treasures in one palace than in all the rest of our lives, we shall go to the opera, drink wine . . ."

Now he was the one—he saw—who thrust his hand in the direction of the other. A different kind of hand.

"And moreover," he said, as if to make his unaccustomed enthusiasm, which by this time had almost assumed the appearance of friendship, immediately ridiculous, "I need you to keep Laura company when I start chasing *real* Italian women."

20

In Rome the writer had put up at the Albergo Nazionale, Sartre's favorite hotel, close to the Piazza Colonna and the Parliament building, which was guarded by carabinieri and a variety of militiamen with submachine guns. It was 1979, after all. The hotel looked as if it could have been there for a hundred years, and he was glad of that, because it gave his sudden departure for Rome at least the semblance of a well-considered decision. Although someone who could conjure up 1879 Bulgaria could surely manage 1979 Rome without actually going there. But never mind, he was here now. Sofia had never appealed to him, and anyway, *they* had left Sofia. They were here, the same as he.

In the Nazionale he had been given room 38, a quiet, sparsely furnished room looking out on a lifeless little courtyard. On the other side of it was a small printing shop from which there came a peaceful sound, as if the chicker-chicker and the doong-doong of the machines were trying to tell him that what he was going to write in that room would be printed before long, a material thing, a book, and afterwards he would have no more to do with it, thank God.

The month was February. The weather was grey but not miserable as in Holland, so he spent much of the time walking. Rome itself had changed little since his last visit ten years ago, and it was still in the process of a prolonged, voluptuous decline, but the atmosphere was tense. Constantly screeching police cars, uniformed men everywhere, with guns and walkie-talkies, doom-laden headlines announcing kidnappings, acts of terrorism, political murders, trials, and a government crisis, but he did not take it to heart any more than the Romans did. Nor did it worry him that everything now closed so much earlier in the evening, and that by eleven o'clock the city center was as dead as a cemetery, for he was back in his room long before that time. After all, he had not come here to amuse himself. Once he thought he saw his friend Inni Wintrop walking near the Vatican and he quickly hid behind one of Bernini's pillars. He did not phone the numbers friends had given him either—he preferred his loneliness because it reinforced his feeling of unreality, for the other writer could say what he liked—and he couldn't run into *him* here, thank God—it still seemed to him that he himself was the fictitious character, a person in a story. He had always had this feeling, even when not writing, and he knew it would always be so. He did not believe it had anything to do with Borges, Pessoa, or any other literary masters; theirs were mere constructions. It was a feeling that belonged to his daily life, perhaps always had. The anxiety that went with it he had learned to suppress, although it remained present as a constant, nagging pain, a physical pressure, but that he put up with without complaint.

He wandered about the Forum Romanum, thinking of those truly real senators, consuls, priests, soldiers, and martyrs, not written by anyone, that had dissolved here into nothingness. History did not offer much to hold on to! The notion of time had always been a mystery to him. With the bland arrogance of the born artsman he had always kept totally away from math and science, and he still regretted it. He would never lose the feeling that some of the most essential things in the world escaped him utterly, that he could not *think*, as he said himself, that he would die ignorant. Whether the point at issue was the origin of the universe or the categorical imperative, immediately a veil would fall between him and the person who was trying to explain something to him; it was not unwillingness on his part but a kind of paralysis that could be traced back to his first math lesson. He had struggled through several books on time during one long summer on a beach in Spain, but to the extent that he had understood them at all, they had not helped much. His approach remained sentimental. He simply thought that time did not exist, that was the easiest way out, or on the contrary, as now, while he looked down on the Forum from the curve in the via San Pietro in Carcere, that time was the only thing that would always exist, the invisible shell inside which everything happened.

There was a faint haze that slightly blurred the reddish soil and the cypresses in the distance; the sun lent a pink glow to some large brick buildings in the vicinity of the Piazza Venezia, to his left. Children played among the carelessly scattered fragments of monuments. Half and whole pillars, pedestals, and capitals lay and stood here and there, and it seemed to him that with these fragments yet another notion of time had fallen to pieces: some parts of it were still standing, others lying, while yet others had simply vanished, and at the same moment he knew that all the time that had ever existed still existed now, and it was precisely the person who reflected upon it who was short of time, because during what was called his life he was allowed to roam around for only this long or that long, in indivisible, unbroken time, until he reached the end of his allotted span and would vanish without a trace. Even the traces among which he was walking now, which put these wandering thoughts into his mind, were no older than a few thousand years, and they would wear away and disappear like the earth itself. Only time would continue to exist. Or would that vanish as well? But then nothing would ever have existed. Slowly he walked down the steps of the Campodoglio, to regain the Forum by a roundabout route.

It was this notion, more than any other thought or figment of the imagination, that made him and the whole world fictitious, because everything was being undermined by future nonexistence, even though at his age, he thought you ought to have grown used to that. At any rate you ought no longer to have any feelings about it, but on the other hand, he thought, still in dialogue with the other writer—who in spite of his absence had clearly just now called him an "unscientific adolescent"—he remained doubtful as to whether this semblance of being, which was the world, ought not to have something as fleeting as genuine semblance added to it.

Sometimes, during those days, sitting on a terrace with a drink or looking at women who—at such moments philosophy is deceived—aroused a very real desire in him, he was quite willing to leave his reflections for what they were, or rather, they left him, but also came back, circling amid the carefree, idly strolling Saturday evening crowd around the illuminated fountain in the Piazza Navona: who were all those people? He saw them as a crowd, more or less happy, gazing at the lions' heads that spat out the water in long silver curves. They embraced and talked together or tried to make contact with one another. They would go to their homes and sleep together. They seemed convinced of the solidity, the visible everlastingness of their city and of those monuments that had existed for so long, so unimaginably long already. And he walked among them and knew that each of them was a story, a book, that would never be written and that after a hundred years they would, in a photograph, look like a nameless, forever vanished crowd in the Piazza Navona, on a February evening in 1979. For the city might be eternal, but they were most definitely not.

"So what," said the other writer, but he could not hear him just now.

21

Lyuben Georgiev's preoccupations were very different, although these, too, were connected with the notion of time. He also was in Rome now, but he had not yet called on the Fičevs. When he thought about it—that is, when he slowly expounded his arguments to himself—he had not done so chiefly because he did not yet wish to "give himself up" to Fičev. He wanted to arrive in his own Rome, not in the Rome where Fičev was in the right, not as a poor guest on a triumphant guided tour. The fact that he did not yet feel up to a confrontation with Laura Fičev was a second consideration. He was afraid something strange and irrevocable might happen, and, not being on his own ground, he first wanted to know where he was. This feeling, which he too now called "being in love," was with him all day, every day, and it had almost reached the point that he no longer needed her for it. He therefore wandered round the city, ill at ease in his civilian clothes, made for him Italian style by the regimental tailor but looking clumsy here, and even too warm for the time of year. He had bought a German guidebook and, with a solemn absence of hurry, picked off the sights one by one, as if it were a military campaign.

At night, in his hotel, he read about the history of the Roman Empire, and in the daytime he saw, in the Forum, what remained of it. Especially the triumphal arches of Titus and Constantine, with their reliefs depicting army units in victorious battles, fascinated him, and that was how, perhaps for the first time in his life, he began to reflect upon time, whereby he came to vaguer, and most of all different, conclusions from those of the writer, with whom his life was now so invisibly and so tenaciously connected.

To Lyuben Georgiev, time simply consisted of history. For as long as there had been people, there had been history. History determined the present, the present the future, and therefore the future would not exist without history. Hence it was important to take note of history. Personal destiny did not seem of such importance. History existed for its own sake, in a way. True, it was made by means of people, but it did not always take account of them. A correct, objective appreciation of the rise and fall of Rome would no doubt make it possible to draw certain lessons that might be useful in the task facing the Bulgarian nation. In that sense he was quite grateful to Stefan Fičev, although he tried to put the thought of the doctor as much as possible out of his mind and avoided the area around the Grand Hotel de Russie where the Fičevs were staying. He prepared himself for a sudden chance encounter, but one possibility he had never thought of was that Fičev would send a telegram to his lodgings in Sofia saying, "Coward where are you," to which his landlady, who knew Fičev well, thinking she was acting correctly, had wired back: "Colonel Georgiev staying in Albergo Il Sole," ironically enough a much more Italian-sounding address than that of the doctor.

Not only, thought the colonel as the doctor suddenly stood before him—thank God without Laura—have I never understood anything of Fičev, but I have never known anything about him. That Fičev would be so offended that he, Lyuben, had been in Rome for a whole week and worse still, that he was enjoying himself, had never occurred to him. Not only did it seem as if he had robbed the doctor of a triumph, but also as if he had thwarted yet other, more secret plans and longings.

More surprising even than this was the fact that the doctor's great Italian dream seemed to have been partially destroyed, because he had not experienced it together with the colonel, as if his pleasure, his excitement, could only be realized through another person, just as he had needed Lyuben to rail at Bulgaria—and, if it did not sound too ridiculous, the colonel thought, to love his wife, as if the relationship did not exist unless there was a witness.

The doctor did not speak in friendly terms of his wife. She was "spoilt," "had seen so much already," was incapable of appreciating Rome or at any rate only capable of appreciating it in the way he would have expected of "someone like that." She was always tired and only wanted to go out in the evenings, when the museums were closed. She was not interested in historical background and had feigned all sorts of ailments and depressions so as not to have to join him on his long daily walks. But now that Lyuben was there, even though, God help us, he had discovered this only through Lyuben's landlady in

Sofia, everything would be different; somehow or other Laura had a soft spot for Lyuben. "I don't know how that can be explained either, but it's gone to her head a bit, hahaha."

But Fičev's customary certainty seemed somewhat weakened; he said he had realized for the first time that even in a country you love passionately, you still remain an outsider forever, and that sounded like a reproach. He thought that the Italians as a people were really rather cynical and pessimistic, and for all their melodious chatter about Garibaldi and Cavour and the great unification of the Italian nation, they were simply a crowd of degenerate descendants of former tribes that had built a city in which these descendants lived, unjustly, in his opinion, like a bunch of decadent bastards in the palace of an ancestor whose name they were not even allowed to bear. And he had discovered another love, another dream for his permanent dissatisfaction: Germany. If only the Germans were permitted to rule over this inheritance!

The colonel, who rather liked the utterly casual manner in which the Romans treated the relics of their past grandeur, said nothing. He had never been under the illusion that he might be anything other than a foreigner, a coarse non-Italian in clumsy, heavy clothes, who moreover could scarcely make himself understood. He had not been disappointed in anything.

After an hour they had no more to say to each other. On the chessboard of their friendship a decisive move had been made, and as neither had made it deliberately, they were not yet sure what it meant. Something had changed. It would of course be simplest to say that something had changed in the power relationship between the two men, that the one showed himself to be weaker than the other had imagined him to be, but that would have to mean that whoever was now the stronger had always been the stronger though without knowing it.

The colonel realized that in a mysterious way—unorthodox, corrupt, unuttered, as in politics, he thought not without contempt—he had been given permission to love Laura Fičev, and that, more than ever before in their friendship, he had received permission to be himself, a Bulgarian in Rome, someone who thought slowly, a strong man suffering from nightmares, who had never been very interested in women and was now for the first time in his life in love, with a woman unlike any other woman, someone—but this was why the permission was in fact superfluous—who had discovered in Fičev a dependence of which neither he nor Fičev had ever been aware.

They agreed to go for a drive at sunset, and that evening Rome tolerated no splendor besides herself, not even that of Laura Fičev. Gently swaying, they sat in the carriage, her weightless hands touched his; she said things into the empty space beside his head where he could not hear her; her gaze dissolved on contact with other statues and monuments than the ones he was looking at.

The setting sun did terrible things to the city, the late light licked obscenely at the buildings and gave to the ochre walls, the zinc water of the Tiber, the marble pillars and steps, a passionate, dark color, voluptuous to the point of being macabre. It hurt him more than the homesickness he had felt when he saw Laura, now so close beside him, for the first time. She was absorbed by the city, she belonged here, in this flowing stage setting of squares, basilicas, palaces, but at the same time, he thought, it was her ruin, because that extraordinariness of hers was here ordinary. There were so many statues here that made empty gestures into the air and looked at nothing with blind eyes, theatrical figures whose mouths, if open as though they were speaking, made no more sound than a fountain.

The colonel would remember this evening forever: the doctor, stiff and silent, brushed by the last light, his white face marked out against the dark back of the coachman, someone who sees for the last time a dream he has dreamt for years, and knows it.

They drove across the Piazza del Popolo, out by the tall gates, up through the Pincio into the woods of the Villa Borghese where the horse's hooves sounded softly on the paths. A light evening haze, the almost imperceptible rustle of the dark trees, shadows of lovers, her unintelligible sentences, sometimes her hand briefly on his, as if a bird had alighted on it, but when he looked there was nothing.

The coachman lit the oil lamps and hummed a tune, and thus they drove into the silent Bulgarian shadows which settled heavily around their small, moving enclave. The sunlight had gone from the sky; it was dark. Coolness rose from the ground like a chilly ghost, and they drove back to Fičev's hotel. The colonel declined an invitation to dine with them, and the doctor did not insist. Lyuben Georgiev wanted to be alone that evening, eat quietly somewhere, and read in bed for a while. He knew how it would all evolve, just as in the war he had always known from which direction the Turks would come, where and when they would attack.

They decided to go all three to the Vatican Museum the following afternoon, but the colonel knew that Fičev would not keep the appointment, that he would find Laura alone in their room, and that he himself would return to Bulgaria that night.

Whether the other two knew this too, he was unable to say, and none of the three saw, when Lyuben Georgiev continued his way alone on foot, that behind the carriage they had just vacated, another one drove off, in which there sat a lonely stranger, whose clothes were a good deal more eccentric than theirs.

22

That night the colonel slept peacefully for the first time in years, but the writer did not. The constant presence of the other three, in a room too small to contain them, had oppressed him all evening, and in addition there was that horrible, sucking emptiness of the century that should lie between their lives and his. He had dined late at Augusteo's in the Via delle Frezze, and his third grappa had been one too many.

Because the colonel's nightmares had been added to his own, his dreams were complex and exhausting, so that he woke up time and again, utterly worn out. What made it worse was the fact that the other writer kept interfering in a totally inexcusable manner, offering all kinds of scenarios for the development of what he called "your story." As in a cinema from which there is no escape, the writer was forced to watch everything: a grand guignol of possibilities, jealousies, revenge, death, love, a rhapsody of nonsense, because everything had already happened. To see Turks dying amid all this and to follow Laura Fičev's soundless figure fluttering around a dark hotel room like a bird, was too much.

He woke up with a splitting headache and the taste of death and nausea in his mouth you get when you take a too-strong sleeping tablet too late at night. The hotel coffee would be of no avail against such odds and he decided not to order his cappuccino in his room, but to have it in Allemagna, preferably followed by a double espresso. Unshaven, he walked past the sentries and journalists in front of the Parliament building in the Piazza Monte Citorio, entered the underground passage which had once played a part in another story by a Dutch writer, and reemerged on the other side of the Via del Corso, by the newspaper kiosk, where he bought a copy of *Il Messagero*, full of revolution, murders, ayatollahs, and blood.

Today, he knew, he would finish his story. What it was worth he was no longer capable of assessing, and he did not know what he feared more: not being able to finish it or the empty, dangerous feeling that would inevitably assail him after he had.

He ate a tramezino, drank his coffees, and returned to his hotel room and the familiar sounds of the printing shop. The walls of his room were yellow and when he sat quietly for a while without moving, he suddenly saw the colonel's back entering through the elegant revolving door of the Grand Hotel de Russie. He must therefore just have missed Fičev, who had left a moment earlier, his face wearing the expression of someone going out to steal something. Now he had to wait, which he did in silence, seated by his desk, at that unique moment in time (then) and space (there) where not only the colonel but he too had an appointment. He heard the voices of the Italian chambermaids in the corridor, but that was in *his* hotel. He felt his stoniness crumbling and he knew he would get up, with a physical pain, and go to the corridor to ask them to make less noise. It was mostly their hard, resounding footsteps on the stone floor that hurt him. At that other moment where he should now be, there were thick carpets in the corridors of large hotels, and not only the footsteps, but also the voices, already softer because of the greater deference of those days, would therefore sound softer.

When he was seated once again at his desk, the mocking giggles in the corridor still held back the contours of the revolving door; it took too long before he was able to enter through it. But where to? Like a desperate lover who has missed his first rendezvous, he let his gaze wander around the large lobby with its potted palms and gold-braided staff, walked into a corridor and back again, up and down the broad marble staircase covered with Persian carpets, and returned to his room.

The writer knew something had gone fatally wrong, and his eyes closed in humiliation; he waited, he did not know for how long, until the revolving door reappeared in its full nineteenth-century splendor of oak and brass. At that moment the cut-glass of the door, which must have been pushed open by a fairly sturdy hand, so fast did it move, caught a flash, and another, a four-fold flash of late afternoon sunlight, and Colonel Lyuben Georgiev stood on the pavement, lighting a Turkish cigarette. The writer looked at the expression on his face, but there seemed to be none.

At that moment the telephone rang. He had received just one call during his stay in this hotel, and that had been for someone else. Before leaving Amsterdam he had agreed with his wife that she would phone him only in an emergency and would on no account give his number to anyone.

There are many different sounds by which the outside world tries to draw our attention via the telephone. Imploring, nostalgic, belligerent—rattles, buzzes, shrill whistles, and they all seem to express something of the message that will come to us presently out of that mechanical nothingness which is what the telephone resembles most. The high-pitched malevolent ringing that now rebounded from the stone walls of his room sounded like the alarm signal in the fire departments in American movies, thought the writer. He rose and picked up the receiver.

"Pronto," he said.

There was laughter at the other end of the line. Across Alsace, the Alps, and Tuscany, he recognized the voice of the other writer.

"Yes," he said, and added immediately, "How did you get my number?"

"Oh dear," said the other writer, "Aren't we important. I explained to your wife that it was very very urgent because there is a lot of money involved, I mean a lot for you."

He paused meaningfully, but the writer said nothing.

The other writer changed his tone somewhat. It now became nonchalant, with at the same time a hint of the big businessman.

"How are you getting on with that story of yours?"

"Why?" asked the writer.

"I'll explain it all to you. I am on the committee for the

Book-week Award this year. As you know, they always print at least a hundred thousand copies. The last one, by Carmiggelt, made three hundred and seventy thousand."

He waited, but the writer kept silent.

"Well," the tone now became slightly more hesitant, "we were discussing various possibilities and then I suddenly thought of that story of yours. Your wife said it was going to be fairly long."

"Ha-hum," said the writer. He saw the meeting before him. Cups of coffee, packets of Stuyvesants, a few colleagues, a few publishers. Immense tedium, feeble jokes, and the quick toss of a name.

"I told the meeting that for the first time in years you are busy on a story again, and they showed a great deal of interest. For you it would be a pot of gold. But the question is, how far have you got, is it finished, how many words is it or will it be?"

The writer said nothing.

"Hallo, hallo," he heard, all the way from Holland.

"Hang on," he said. He stood up, put the receiver on the bed for a moment, went to his desk and with rapid movements tore the roughly forty sheets on which he had written his story by hand, into long strips, ripped these up once more and threw them into the wastebasket. Then he returned to the bed and picked up the receiver again.

"I have to tell you something," he said. "It is very kind of you and of course I hope I am not making things awkward for you, but obviously I couldn't have foreseen this, or I would never have let it get this far."

"What wouldn't you . . ."

But the writer did not listen. He felt a deadly fatigue, as if he had been tramping through mud for weeks. In a slow, almost lecturing tone he continued, "That story you are talking about does not exist. I am sorry."

"But your wife said . . ."

"My wife is in the same position as you. She doesn't always know what I do and don't do."

Between Holland and Italy there hung a heavy silence.

"Oh, I see," said the other writer. "Well thanks very much." And then, incredulously: "So, er, all that about Bulgaria and so on, that was just nonsense?"

"No," said the writer, "Bulgaria exists."

"Jesus, I mean, that doctor, that colonel, did you just make that up?"

"If I had written it, I would have made it up all the same, according to you," said the writer.

"Oh my God," said the voice from Holland. "So it was all nothing but air?"

"You might call it that," said the writer. "Sorry." And he rang off.

He sat still for a while. Then he went to the wastebasket and started burning the shreds, one by one.

23

About a hundred years earlier, but in the same city, Colonel Lyuben Georgiev, after having been to bed with the wife of his friend Fičev, felt, as he came out of the revolving door of the Grand Hotel de Russie and walked back toward his hotel to catch the evening train to Sofia, a tearing, burning pain in his heart, which he attributed to the past month's events that had, on that afternoon, been concluded in the only way possible.

The doctor and his wife, who were at that moment not at the same place in that city, also thought they knew the reason for the mysterious, burning pain that rent them for one terrible moment and left them breathless. Laura Fičev even thought she was going to die, and perhaps she was right.

24

The idea of the black hole, matter piled up so densely somewhere in the cosmos that nothing can escape from it, had always seemed very poetical to the writer. Having heard that the March number of the *New Scientist* contained a long article on the occasion of Einstein's hundredth birthday, in which black holes came under discussion once again, he had bought a copy. But what struck him even more, in connection with the events of the past month, was a limerick, somewhere in the middle of the article on Einstein. It went like this:

> *There was a young lady named Bright*
> *Who traveled much faster than light*
> *She left home one day*
> *In a relative way,*
> *And came home the previous night.*

Without being able to explain it, he knew that something like this had happened to him. But to whom could he have explained it if he could not understand it himself?

Amsterdam/Rome, summer 1978 / spring 1979

MUNDO:	¿Quién me llama,
	que desde el duro centro
	de aqueste globo que me esconde dentro
	alas visto veloces?
	¿Quién me saca de mí, quién me da voces?
AUTOR:	Es tu Autor Soberano.
	De mi voz un suspiro, de mi mano
	un rasgo es quien te informa
	y a tu oscura materia le da forma.
MUNDO:	Pues ¿qué es lo que mandas? ¿Qué me quieres?
AUTOR:	Pues soy tu Autor, y tú mi hechura eres
	hoy, de un concepto mío
	la ejecución a tus aplausos fío.

Don Pedro Calderón de la Barca
El Gran Teatro del Mundo, 1655

WORLD: Who calls me here on speedy wing?
Whose mighty voice has bidden
Me leave the earth's deep womb where I lay
hidden?
DIRECTOR: Your Maker and your Lord.
For it was I that poured
My breath into the air to raise you, I that fanned
You into form with my own hand.
WORLD: What orders then? How wilt Thou be obeyed?
DIRECTOR: I being your Maker, you the thing I made,
I now wish to employ
You in a thing invented for my joy.

Don Pedro Calderón de la Barca
The Great Stage of the World
Translated by George W. Brandt
(Manchester University Press, 1976)